PREVAILED HOPE

Daniel Paice

Copyright © 2021 Daniel Paice

Prevailed Hope by Daniel Paice

Published by Daniel Paice

Copyright ©
2021
Daniel Paice

ISBN: 9798520072973

All rights reserved. No portion of this book may be reproduced in any form without the permission of the publisher, except as permitted by the U.K. copyright laws.

For permissions, contact: DanielPaiceWriter@gmail.com

To Hope, a friend and colleague who, without perhaps realising it, restored my faith in my writing during some of the toughest years of my life.

CONTENTS

Title Page
Copyright
Dedication
Introduction

PART 1	1
Hello, Sadness	3
The Burn of Lost Pride	4
I Didn't Choose to be this Way	5
Internal Massacre	6
A Chance at Healing	7
A Fleeting Moment	8
Tears of Sadness, They Bleed	9
Tomorrow's Dawn	10
Away we Fly	11
PART 2	13
Times are Changing	14
I Rose Above You	15
A Bond Forever Broken	16
In Loathing, There is no Love	17
Losing the Ones you Love is a Tender Thing	18
Ghostly Thoughts	20
To be a Warrior	21
'X' Marks the Spot	22

We must Fight, Always	23
PART 3	25
Hope is a Powerful Thing	26
Deep in the Night	27
The Art of Life	28
The Next Adventure	29
A Canvas	30
Kindness	31
Creativity is My Advocate	32
The Sun Finally Shines	33
About The Author	35

INTRODUCTION

If you are reading these words, I thank you. It really means a lot to think that even ten people could read my work. Thank you for taking a chance on me.

Writing a book is no mean feat - no matter how many pages, words, or the genre of the book itself. And that's without wondering whether that sentence (or, in this case, line) looks or sounds right, only to delete it and start again. Wondering whether what you've written makes any sense at all.

My job as a writer is to make a reader *feel*, and from what I've been told, this anthology certainly delivers. Throughout the anthology, we'll be exploring several aspects of mental health and the different stages of recovery, all derived from my own experiences. And, of course, the fact that there is hope to be found in any situation - it might just take you a while, and several attempts more, to find it.

Your reading this means my job is, for now, complete. So I now pass the reins over to you, in the hope that you find at least one line of this entire book enjoyable; that the messages you come across will resonate with you in some way, and help you better manage any struggles you may (or may not) be going through. That would mean the world to me. Those of you that have read my blog, The Sanity Mentality, will understand where my passion for mental health awareness comes from...

A little side note before you continue: although the writing is more hopeful towards the end of the book, this is not a light-hearted read. There are references to depression, anxiety, suicidal ideation, PTSD and death throughout. If this is triggering for you, then perhaps this isn't the book for you.

Nonetheless, it is a good read!

All the best,

Daniel Paice

P.S. If you could please leave a review on Amazon, once you've read it, that would be massively appreciated.

PART 1

Midnight

HELLO, SADNESS

Hello, Sadness,
how nice of you to show up.
My only certainty,
what a pity,
even in an uncertain future.
Which is more than I can say
for the torture of life.

Give me a drink or two and
I'll feel even lower,
But that's okay because
you've given me all I've ever wanted.
A deep, dark well.

It's deep, dark walls
keep the laborious talons of life
at bay.
Which is more than I can say
for my mind; echoing
in its very own sorrow
unable to escape the talons of life.
Please, just give me a moments' peace.

THE BURN OF LOST PRIDE

When you lose your pride,
it hurts to be alive.
Nothing to do but feel the hot pain
wash over you.
Nothing you can do,
but await your social sentence of shame,
so you sit patiently.

Sit patiently in that hour of a second.
Not sure what's happening -
not even sure if it is happening.
Grappling at your heart,
Begging.
For once,
not to feel the heat
of those dangerous eyes
Piercing your skin like owls in the night.

Being the fool, you believe in the blooming hope.
Just for once, and never again.

So you sit patiently, knowing full well it hurts to be alive.
Hoping this moment stays in the past.

I DIDN'T CHOOSE TO BE THIS WAY

It's not like I chose to be this way.
I kept my life in order,
my friends close.
I kept my head in check, as far as anybody is concerned.
Simple,
happy,
me.

Building a wall so tall
you can't see me anymore,
too ashamed and suffocated
to even negotiate with my own thoughts,
as they whirl like a tornado, slowly destroying my mind.
And yet here I am, functioning,
as normal people do.
A projection of who I am supposed to be.

You can't see me; the real me, but I can.
Pain seeping through my veins,
absorbing it better than ever before,
trying to heal.
But the damage is done.

So Think,
Before you judge.
It could be you;
crumbling under your doleful thoughts,
functioning as normal people do.

INTERNAL MASSACRE

I pay too much for this vessel of mine,
trapped within a cell,
hidden from the world.
Where a stale beast shines so brightly on the outside,
festering on the inside.
Where *'fine'* couldn't be further from the truth.

Putting myself back together with sticks and stones,
my bones having already broken.
One by one
the foundations fail,
the weight of resentment
crushing me flat.
Being strangled by
Hatred,
Shame,
and Guilt.

How long can this really go on?
Battling to keep my composure
with the walls tumbling,
and the ceiling crumbling.
Every day it is the same battle,
Only to be asked why I didn't fix it with a smile.

A CHANCE AT HEALING

On another occasion,
I might actually be able to tell you how I feel,
perhaps even heal.
But not now.
Not ever.
That was made certain.

On another occasion,
I might be able to tell you where to find the meaning of life.
But somehow, for some reason,
That's all irrelevant right now,
Forever.

On an occasion such as this,
I can tell you the meaning of both life and death.
One minute your heart is burning bright.
The next, your heart is weighed down by death.
I realise that now.
They work simultaneously, you see.

But right now I must go,
I'll see you on the other side.
If you just let go.

A FLEETING MOMENT

Only when a
moment has passed, do you
realise how much it meant.

Only when you
can't do anything, do you
realise how much
damage you've done.

Only when
A precious soul
stands before you,
do you realise how much
you could have done,
you haven't done,
and what you should have done.

After all they've done for me,
are the murderous glances,
and the aggressive silences
the best that I can do?

TEARS OF SADNESS, THEY BLEED

Sadness is a funny thing,
almost ironic.
Contagious, like a disease.
You're always told to be strong
when you really can't.
As though to keep it all in,
to see how much you can stand,
Until the end.
Thick tears, they bleed
from your eyes,
no matter how hard you
fight to hold off the ambush.
As the lies of happiness
come flooding in,
only to test
the last of your dignity.

TOMORROW'S DAWN

When tomorrow's dawn comes,
and I'm not there to see,
remember me.

Don't cry until the early hours,
don't cry and cower away.
Don't try and save me,
just remember me the way I was,
I'll say good-bye the right way.

When tomorrow's dawn comes,
Look under the hedgerow.
Past where the pumpkins grow,
where the Well makes its presence.
That's where the explanations repose.

Who am I to even assume you'll
notice me gone?
I am hardly the life and soul of the party.

AWAY WE FLY

Away we fly,
away up high,
skimming the brim of life.
Our time is up,
for we must die.

Our souls are
The whispers in the wind,
tangling you in your pain,
as a way of saying 'hi,' or
the calling of
the rain.
But that's okay,
because now we are free.

PART 2

DAWN

TIMES ARE CHANGING

Times are changing,
that much is clear,
as we watch
the leaves on the trees change
with the passing of time.

The relationships that seem to be held
in a permanent stronghold
are now held in the grasp of fickle fingers.
Everything could be for nothing,
Nothing could be for everything.
I don't hold the answers,
nobody does, not really.
Only time will tell.

But what I do know is that
relationships are the foundations
of everything we hold dear.
And even the things not so much,
because without either or,
would we really appreciate the things we do indeed hold dear?

Would we understand the value that their existence
encompasses?
That's for us, and our innate intuition, to decide.

I ROSE ABOVE YOU

I see those frivolous glances.
You think me weak,
that I don't see.
But you should feel the squirming scream
that nests within me.
A memory is the price to pay
for the days of affection - that's
all you could afford.

I sat, humming a tune,
knowing that fate will find me,
take me away on the journey
of a lifetime.
But I guess it's time to go our separate ways
and say Goodbye.

A BOND FOREVER BROKEN

If only my heart had been big enough,
perhaps I would have held onto the love you gave to me.
But sooner or later it was going to go wrong,
overflow, spill into unknown territory.

Perhaps now that my head is clearing,
we could foster the bond
that once broke with a brittle snap,
during a moment you never noticed.

IN LOATHING, THERE IS NO LOVE

Look at you,
eyes hollow, soul shallow.
I was sold on the promise of affection,
not the promise of death.
I saw right through you.

In loathing there is no love,
only hate,
as you bore me with
the schemes and dreams
that'll surely be your demise.

A bond tends to go both ways, you see.
One day there won't be any energy left to
drain with your delusions.

LOSING THE ONES YOU LOVE IS A TENDER THING

Losing the ones you love,
whatever which way,
is a tender thing.

Whether they are in your life for an hour,
or the long haul,
they are a lifeline.
We are a lifeline,
strung up by hopefully hundreds
wishing us well,
giving us the support we need.

So when one lets us down,
we feel the fall,
feel the pain.
We were expecting them to
show the same loyalty we showed them,
but sadly that's not to be.

So whether we've hit a brick wall,
or allowed them to pass on by,
we must move on,
and boogie to the groove of life.
It's sad to think how fast life can pass by,
whether we were having fun.
Whether we were paying attention or not.
Without saying Goodbye.

Everything comes second to time.
Except perhaps the present moment, they are in kahoots.
Or so I'm told.

And yet us humans are all above that,
forever in the past.
Until the past catches up with the future.

GHOSTLY THOUGHTS

I'm sorry, but in being a lone traveller,
try as I may,
I can only take one of these paths.
All of which, are veering this way and that;
what am I supposed to do with that?

If I wander aimlessly, I'll get lost,
Lonely at night with my own Empty, Ghostly thoughts,
shrinking in fear with nowhere to go.
I won't be able to escape this eternal cycle,
you and I both know that.

Your only option?
Build a path of your own graph,
avoiding social oppression with every block.
That way, my friend, is the way to go.
Those that will try to stop you are not worth your time.

TO BE A WARRIOR

To be a warrior you need
to be prepared to fall;
be able to pick up the pieces, and
reorder your failures
into one big success -
that's what makes you strong.

Keep it together, they say.
But in order to heal,
you have to let go,
recognise when that feeling is
doing you a disservice.

It will get better,
however long it takes,
you will have success.
It's the way of life,
to question who you want to be,
and who you will be.
That's what makes you stronger.

'X' MARKS THE SPOT

We start life unknowing, innocent.
Almost like a dead man walking,
a blind man reading,
a cacophony of noise clouding our judgement;
stuffing our ears with hyperreality.

A journey in which we have no map.
Not even an 'X' marks the spot.
No dotted line of which to pin our hopes.
The only certainty of
racing to the end of the road.
Trusting in our perfect imperfections;
constantly monitored by the eyes of society.
Trusting that we are going in the right direction.

And even when we've completed life's arduous sentence,
we keep up the pretence.
So certain as we are,
that we're all here of our own free will.

<u>WE MUST FIGHT, ALWAYS</u>

The pages of my story are getting thinner by the day,
weakened and weathered by ambush.
But whilst there is still life in my lungs,
and blood in my veins,
the fight will go on.
As it must,
as it always will.

PART 3

MIDDAY

HOPE IS A POWERFUL THING

I feel a burst of hope,
I will fulfil my dreams.
The happy thoughts are no longer coming in
dribs and drabs,
they are a blossoming flower.

A man on the brink of death,
having found life again.
It's a wonderful feeling
to be the driving force,
thriving in your very own life.
Oh, what a wonderful thing.

They say nothing in life ever
comes easy.
Only from going to hell and back,
do I understand what that means.

Only from going to hell and back,
do we realise what a pleasure
it is to live life on the sunny side.

Respectfully building our funds and foundations
so we never have to go there again,
because we know it would kill us if we did.

It's now our duty to guide others through
these depths of darkness.

DEEP IN THE NIGHT

Deep in the night, we are lost in our thoughts.
Into the woods we go,
the stars shining brightly
in our wake.
As we pass each milestone with a wave,
each one bigger than the last,
we are more experienced.
We have learned,
whether from all our mistakes,
or just one or two,
the milestones that once towered above us
now shrink in our wake.

THE ART OF LIFE

There is a technique, an art,
to finding your own way.
And just like art,
the lesson in life takes time to learn,
to develop,
patience to master,
and skill to nurture,
and courage to carry on.

Those of us that do, find the beauty and hope
in the most concentrated darkness.
Even when there's nobody
ready to welcome you home,
with open arms and a loving heart.

Home from your long journey
of self discovery,
of finding the internal strength
you never feel until you need it most.
A monotonous symphony willing you on
with your desires in mind.

Be proud of yourself, you made it here.
Nobody else could have carried you, only guided you.

THE NEXT ADVENTURE

Death is an opening,
a release into another world.
Ready in waiting to start your
next big adventure,
the next line in the narrative of the universe.
Make your mark,
a line is all you've got.
Speak it loud and clear,
for all the world to hear.

A CANVAS

An experience, good or bad,
will make its way onto the unmarked page
in an explosion of colour and prose.
A canvas marked forever.

A good experience is in measure of the bad.
Pain at our expense, delves deep into the soul,
reminding us to make the best of the better.
Reminding us there will always be
a force for good to oppose every bad.

A writer's solace is the place to be.
Infinite worlds to explore,
feelings to express,
scars to outcast.

There's only happiness here,
where the catharsis resides.

KINDNESS

Other people's kindness can make you cry.
Kindness can hurt,
touching the deepest depths of our heart.

People forget the act of kindness,
but they never forget the feeling of kindness striking their heart,
the truth and sincerity that flooded their veins.
Gratitude is a powerful thing,
So hold kindness close to your heart.
Because with that kindness,
given or received,
we are invincible.

CREATIVITY IS MY ADVOCATE

Creativity ebbs and flows,
resonates like a welcomed light,
above all the rest,
when life puts us to the test.

Creativity is my advocate
when all seems lost.
I can trust in my instincts,
the unlimited power my mind
and pen wield.

Together they are unstoppable,
a force to be reckoned with,
just like me.

THE SUN FINALLY SHINES

The sun is definitely brighter
when you've been in the dark so long.

No sir, never going in there again.
Me and my thoughts are not lovers,
or friends even, no sir they are not.
But an even keel might still be possible.
A black mind is not always a black heart,
so we keep the blood pumping,
our spirit flowing.

It's a wonderful thing,
to feel your chest burning
with passion and determination.
Finally slowing down the perpetual anger and hatred.

A welcome change,
like the changing of the seasons,
or the symphonic cohesion of
Sunlight and Moonlight weather.
Playing God with your own life.
Oh, what a wonderful feeling.

The walls are no longer crumbling and tumbling,
but building themselves stronger than ever,
full of appreciation.

ABOUT THE AUTHOR

Daniel Paice

Daniel Paice is a writer living in England, using his voice to help and entertain people.

When he is not working on personal writing projects, Daniel is a freelance copywriter and mental health blogger. As he is currently still in part-time education, he does like to keep himself busy with these side-hustles - with the intention of writing one day becoming his full-time occupation.

If you would like to keep updated on his latest 'entrepreneurial and writing endeavours', here is where to find him:

Twitter: @DanJWrites
LinkedIn: Daniel Paice
Blog: The Sanity Mentality